This Belongs to:
Nickolas W. Dery
Ryan A. Williamson

Waldo presents

Totally Bored Boris!

Have you ever had a day when you felt really bored? When you were even too bored to play with your friends or read a book?

I know what those days are like! What makes it worse is when nobody pays any attention to you or sees how bored you are. That can really make you angry—and *that* can make you feel like teasing or fighting.

Boris, the little bear in our story, has a day like this. He can't think of anything to do. He doesn't want to play with his little sister or her friends. But his attempt to bother them turns out very differently from what he had expected!

Your friend,

Waldo

A MERRITALES™ Book

Totally Bored Boris!

Written and illustrated by
Hans Wilhelm

GROLIER ENTERPRISES CORP.

Manufactured in the United States of America   2   3   4   5   6   7   8   9   0

Boris had played with all of his toys. He had read all of his books. But now he didn't know what to do next. He thought and thought. But he could think of nothing to do.

Boris was totally bored.

Finally Boris got up and went to his father. He tooted his trumpet and said, "Let's do something."

"I am doing something," said his father. "I'm busy painting. Why don't you go fishing?"

"Fishing is no fun to do alone," said Boris. "Please do something with me."

"I can't right now," said his father. "Why don't you read a book?"

"I'm tired of my books!" replied Boris.

Boris hoped that his mother would do something with him.

"I'd love to," said his mother, "but I promised your little sister I'd bake some cookies with her. Why don't you help us?"

"No, no, *no!*" cried Boris. "I hate my sister—and I hate baking cookies!"

And he stomped back to his room.

Boris could hear happy
noises coming from the
kitchen. The chattering and
laughing made him feel even
worse. He decided to go to
his tree house.

"Maybe there's something to play with there," he said. He took his trumpet with him, just in case there wasn't.

But as soon as Boris had climbed up the tree, he saw that there was nothing to do. It was as boring as being back in his room.

"What can I do?
What can I do?" he
asked himself over
and over again.

There were lots of
things he *didn't* want
to do—but nothing
that he *really* wanted
to do.

Suddenly a huge cardboard box came walking by.
From inside came the voice of Boris's sister chanting,
"I'm on my way to build a castle. But no one will know
where it is. It's a secret!"

From his tree Boris could see exactly where she was going. "Building a castle!" he thought. "What a boring idea. If *I* had that box, I'd make a spaceship out of it!"

He kept watching as his sister and her friends began their work.

Soon Boris saw everyone pasting cutouts and buttons on the castle and painting pictures on the walls.

Boris knew what he would have done instead. A spaceship would need rockets and aerials and lots of other things.

But then he remembered that he was much too bored to do anything anyway.

The next thing Boris saw was his sister and her friends carrying streamers and crepe paper.

"I guess they're going to have a party," Boris thought. "So what! I hate parties!"

But he kept watching them from his tree house.

"Mother gave us all her old jewelry and clothes to play dress-up in," his little sister said very loudly as she passed under Boris's tree a few minutes later. "I'll be a princess. But you won't see it!" she added.

Of course he would see it, Boris thought to himself—and he acted as if he weren't even interested.

The dressing up sounded very noisy and cheer-ful.

Boris imagined what he would dress up as, if it were his party—a spaceman, or even an alien from a strange planet!

But then Boris saw that the others were having a good time anyway. That made him feel more out-of-sorts than ever.

When they posed so the princess could take a snapshot, Boris threw twigs down at them. But they were having too good a time to notice.

Then his sister said to her friends, "Now let's have a party—oh, no, I mean a royal feast!"—remembering that she was now a princess.

She walked proudly by Boris's tree again, this time carrying a bowl filled with warm cookies.

The sweet smell of the freshly baked cookies drifted up to Boris's tree house. The pitcher of juice made him feel thirsty. But nobody paid any attention to him. They were too busy laughing, eating, and having a good time together.

"This is too much!" said Boris.

Boris couldn't bear it any longer. He
picked up his trumpet and blew it as loud
as he could. *Bwaat!*
Then again. And again! *Bwaat! Bwaat!*

When he stopped,
there was silence! There
was no talking or
giggling. The trumpet
noise had worked! It had
put an end to their silly
fun and stupid party.
Boris felt very pleased
with himself.

But suddenly he heard
his name called from
below.

"Boris, a trumpeter is just what a royal feast needs!" called one of the guests. "How about it? Will you be the king's trumpeter?"

Boris was about to say something very rude. But then he thought for a moment and said, "Maybe I *could* be the trumpeter. But I'll only do it if I get twenty cookies!"

"How about three?" asked his sister, looking at the almost empty bowl.

"Okay," said Boris, "that's a fair price." And he climbed down from the tree.

The party turned out to be fantastic! The trumpeter trumpeted. The king drummed. The royal court danced. And Boris forgot all about his boredom and nothing-to-dos.

But he did *not* forget about the cookies which the princess had saved especially for him.